For my friend and illustrator
extraordinaire, Pat Schories!
—A.S.C.

Biscuit Meets the Class Pet Text copyright © 2010 by Alyssa Satin Capucilli Illustrations copyright © 2010 by Pat Schories All rights reserved. No part of this book may be used or reproduced in any manner whatsoever without written permission except in the case of brief quotations embodied in critical articles and reviews. Manufactured in China. For information address HarperCollins Children's Books, a division of HarperCollins Publishers, 195 Broadway, New York, NY 10007.
www.icanread.com

Library of Congress Cataloging-in-Publication Data
Capucilli, Alyssa Satin, date
  Biscuit meets the class pet / by Alyssa Satin Capucilli ; illustrated by Pat Schories. — 1st ed.
    p. cm. — (My first I can read)
  Summary: When Nibbles, the class pet, gets lost during a visit, Biscuit the puppy helps find him.
  ISBN 978-0-06-117747-7 (trade bdg.) — ISBN 978-0-06-117749-1 (pbk.)
  [1. Dogs—Fiction. 2. Animals—Infancy—Fiction. 3. Rabbits—Fiction.] I. Schories, Pat, ill. II. Title.
PZ7.C179Bislm 2010   2008044032
[E]—dc22   CIP
                                                                                                              AC

18 19 20   SCP   10 9   ❖   First Edition

Biscuit Meets the Class Pet

story by ALYSSA SATIN CAPUCILLI

pictures by PAT SCHORIES

HARPER

An Imprint of HarperCollinsPublishers

Here, Biscuit.

Come meet Nibbles!

Woof, woof!

This is Nibbles.

Nibbles is our class pet.

Nibbles is here for a visit.

Woof, woof!

Hop, hop!

Look, Biscuit!

Nibbles found your bone.

Woof, woof!

Hop, hop!

Nibbles found your ball.

Woof, woof!

Hop, hop!

Nibbles found your bed, too!

Woof!
Silly puppy!
No tugging.

Stay here, Biscuit.
I will get a snack
for Nibbles.

Woof, woof!

Hop, hop!

Woof!

Hop, hop!

Woof!

Hop, hop!

Woof, woof! Woof, woof!

Hop!

21

Oh no, Biscuit!

Where is Nibbles?

Woof, woof!

We must find him.

Woof, woof!

Nibbles is not under the table.

Woof, woof!

Nibbles is not on the chair.

Woof, woof!

Where can Nibbles be?

Woof, woof!
Sweet puppy!

Nibbles found your bone
and your ball
and your bed!

Woof, woof!
And you found Nibbles.
Woof!